There's an Alien

IN YOUR BOOK

Written by TOM FLETCHER

Illustrated by GREG ABBOTT

For Max – T.F.

For Annika – G.A.

PUFFIN BOOKS

UK | USA | Canada | Ireland | Australia | India | New Zealand | South Africa

Puffin Books is part of the Penguin Random House group of companies whose
addresses can be found at global.penguinrandomhouse.com.

www.penguin.co.uk
www.puffin.co.uk
www.ladybird.co.uk

First published 2019

001

Copyright © Tom Fletcher, 2019
Illustrated by Greg Abbott

The moral right of the author has been asserted

Printed in China

A CIP catalogue record for this book is available from the British Library

ISBN: 978–0–241–35720–0

All correspondence to:
Puffin Books, Penguin Random House Children's, 80 Strand, London WC2R 0RL

OH NO!

A spaceship has crash-landed in your book!

What a lot of smoke!
I think there's something there . . .

Blow the smoke away
and turn the page . . .

AAAARGH! It's an ALIEN!

Look at that big round head . . . yuck!

And those wibbly-wobbly antennae . . . double yuck!

And all those slimy suckers . . .
yuck, yuck, **Yuck!**

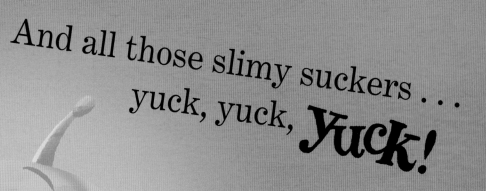

Make your scariest face and shout . . .
Go away, Alien!

OH NO!

It's crying . . .
Perhaps we shouldn't have been so mean.

Pat the alien's head to make it feel better.

That's better – look, it's smiling!
(I don't know what it's saying, though – do you?)

Now we need to help Alien get back
up into space. But . . .

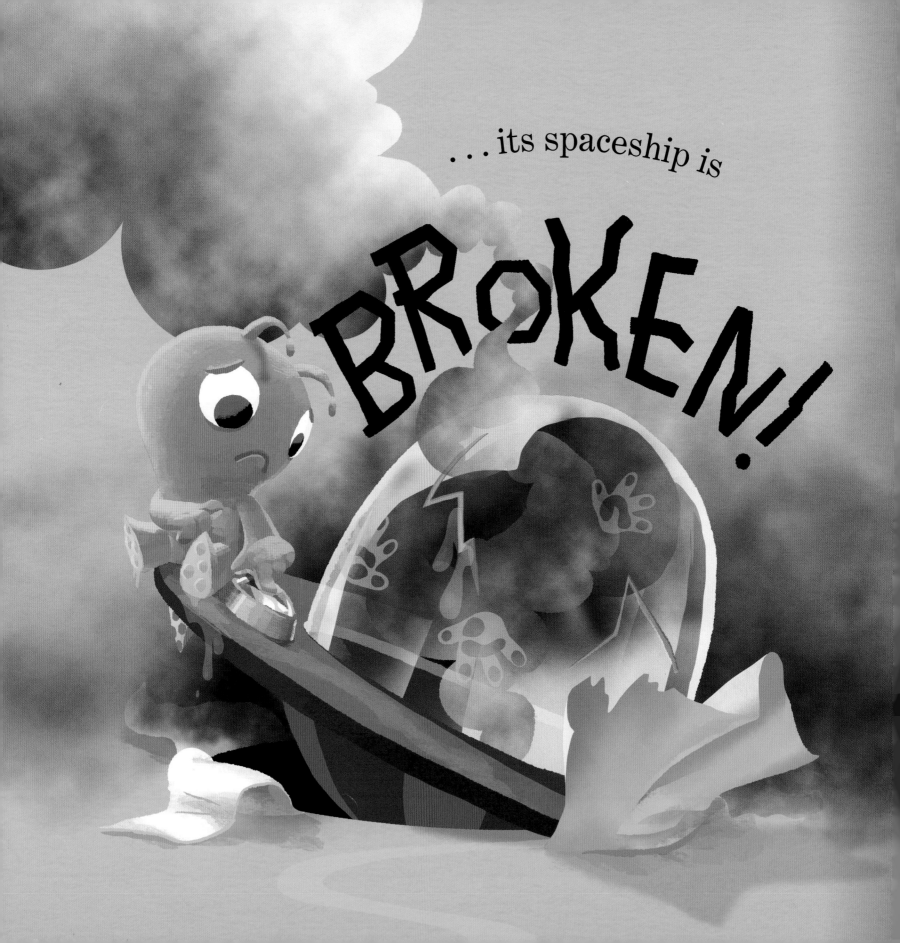

We'll have to find another way.

JIGGLE the book UP and DOWN –
that might bounce it back into space . . .

Wow! You bounced Alien high,
but not high enough.

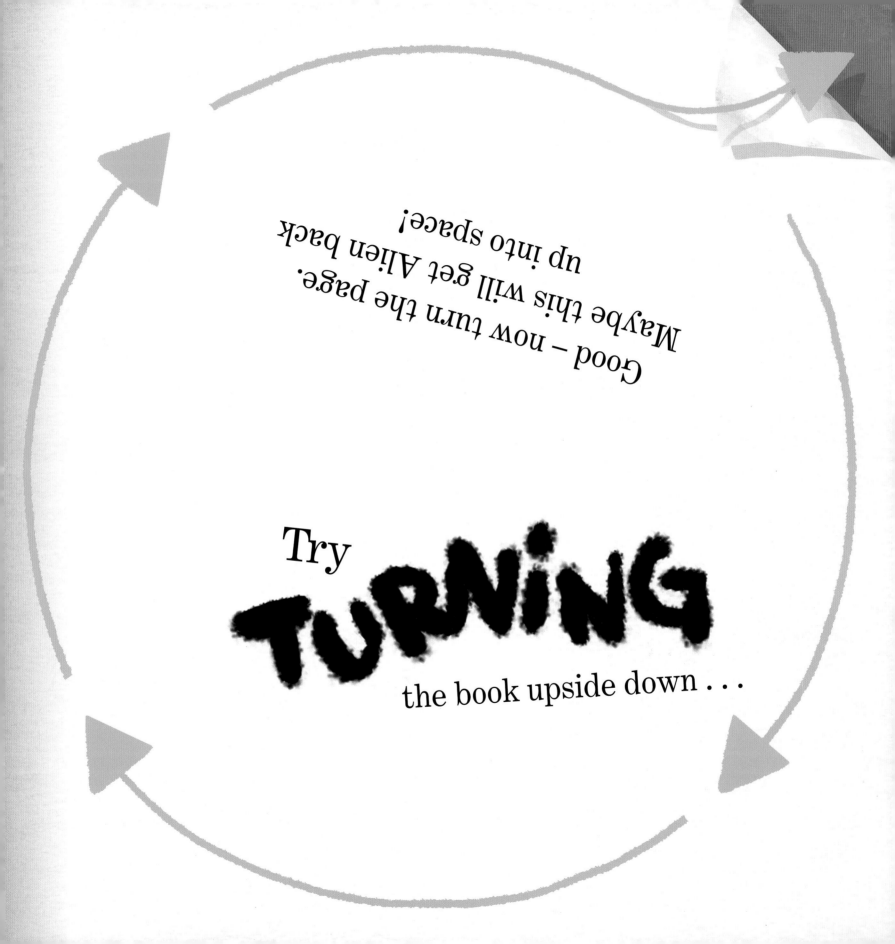

Try TURNING the book upside down . . .

Good – now turn the page.
Maybe this will get Alien back
up into space!

Look! Alien is standing on its head –
but it's not in space!

Try **LIFTING** the book **HIGH** up
in the air and turn the page . . .

UH-OH!

Alien's very high up,
but it's STILL not in space –
and it looks a little scared . . .

Phew!

Alien's safe
back on the
ground.

But aliens don't belong on Earth – they're much too different.

Earth is for people . . . and pugs . . .
frogs and bugs,
fish and snails,
bees and whales!

Close your eyes and **IMAGINE** these creatures to show Alien why it doesn't belong here.

Hang on –
all those things look pretty different too!

Alien, you've got boggly eyeballs,
wibbly-wobbly antennae
and skin sloppier than a slug, but . . .

we're **all** weird and wonderful . . .

So you're welcome to stay here on Planet Earth!

Now, if Alien is going to stay,
I think it needs a home in this book.

Use your finger to draw a house shape here,
then close your eyes, say **zaa-zee-zoo**,
and turn the page . . .

That looks like the

perfect

home!

Hmm – I think Alien needs a friend to play with.

Shout ...

Come and be friends with Alien!
as loudly as you can.

Well done! It worked!
You called a friendly little monster.

I think he'll make a great friend for Alien
– don't you?

And Monster has a surprise for Alien . . .

He's fixed the spaceship!
Now they are ready for an . . .

Adventure!

Press the button on the spaceship and count down – 5, 4, 3, 2, 1 . . .

LIFT OFF!
Wave goodbye to Alien and Monster and say . . .

zaa-zee-zoo!